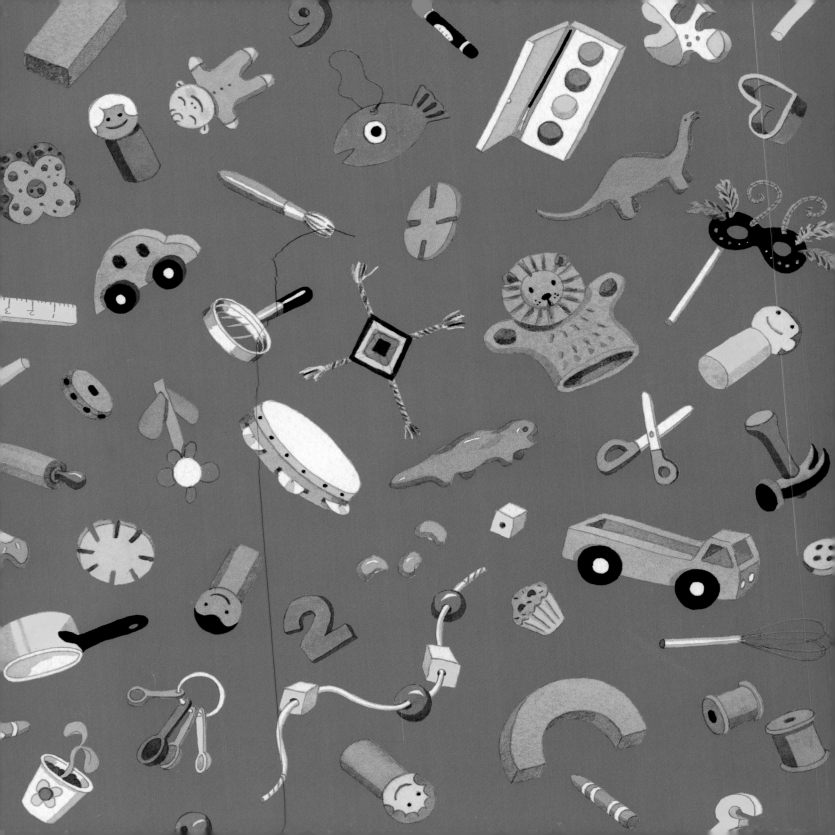

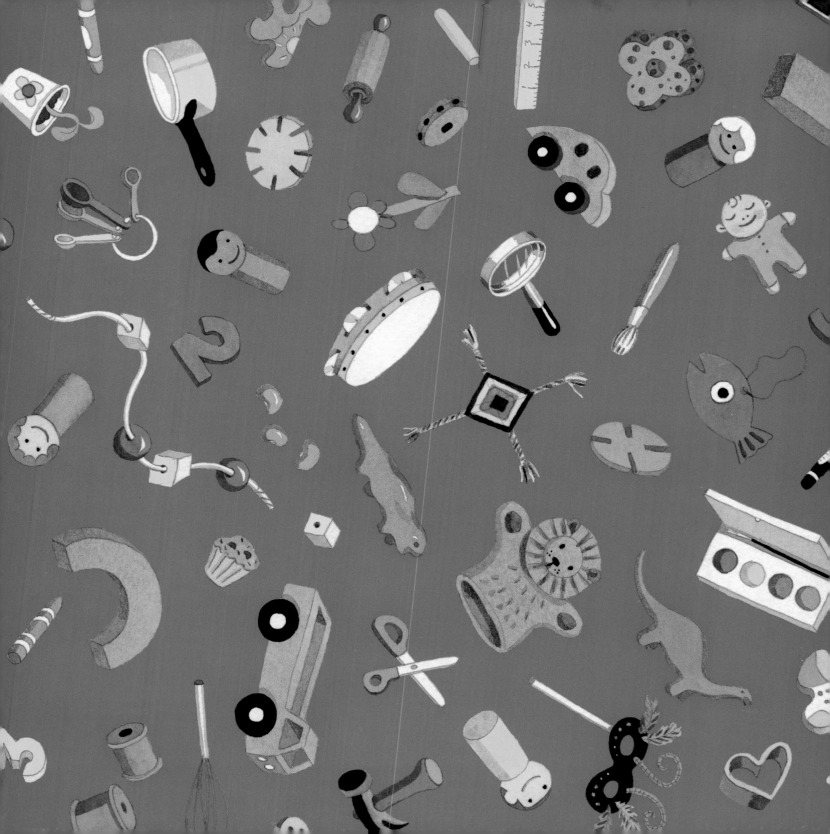

Valentine's Day

story by ANNE ROCKWELL

pictures by LIZZY ROCKWELL

HarperCollinsPublishers

Valentine's Day
Text copyright © 2001 by Anne Rockwell   Illustrations copyright © 2001 by Lizzy Rockwell   Manufactured in China
All rights reserved. For more information, visit us at our web site at www.harperchildrens.com.
Library of Congress Cataloging-in-Publication Data   Rockwell, Anne F.   Valentine's Day / story by Anne Rockwell ; pictures by
Lizzy Rockwell.   p.   cm.   Summary: The children in Mrs. Madoff's class make special Valentine's cards to send to a friend in Japan
and to share at their classroom celebration.   ISBN 0-06-027794-7 — ISBN 0-06-028515-X (lib. bdg.) — ISBN 0-06-051183-4 (pbk.)
[1. Valentine's Day—Fiction.   2. Schools—Fiction.]   PZ7.R943Val   2001   97-17492   [E]—dc21   CIP   AC
Typography by Elynn Cohen ❖

For Isabelle Madeleine Madoff
—A. R. and L. R.

Today is going to be a busy day at school.
We're making valentines for a special friend.

We need a lot of things
to make our valentines with.
Mrs. Madoff and Mr. Siscoe
help us with our messages.

Mine says,
"Please be my valentine.
I miss you. Mrs. Kelley misses you, too.
Love, Sam."

Nicholas makes one that says,
"I want you to be my valentine because
you always let me take a turn on the slide,
and you never push or shove."

Sarah's valentine is pink.
Her valentine says,
"I miss you every single day,
especially when it's snack time."

Charlie draws an airplane
on his valentine.
He loves airplanes.
Charlie wishes he could ride
on an airplane, too.

Jessica wrote a poem.
It says,
"I love you.
Your shoes are blue,
And mine are too."
I like the way "you" rhymes with
"blue" and "too."

Evan writes his name all by himself
in fancy red letters.

Eveline puts a line of gold glitter glue
around the edge of a big red paper heart.
She pastes lace and lots of shiny stickers on it.
"I'm making a super-special valentine," she says,
"because she gave me such a super-special
birthday present."

Pablo's valentine has a picture
of a happy fish.
It says,
"Will you be my valentine?
Your friend, Pablo."

Kate's valentine is a picture
of red and heart-shaped flowers.
There's a kite in the sky, too.

After we put our valentines in a big envelope,
Mrs. Madoff writes the address on it.

We walk to the post office together.

Mrs. Madoff gives
the postal worker
some money,
and she gives Mrs. Madoff
enough stamps to send
our big envelope
all the way to Japan.

On Wednesday, we decorate a big box.
Thursday is Valentine's Day.
Each of us brings one valentine to school.
We drop our valentines in the secret box.
It doesn't matter which of my friends picks mine.

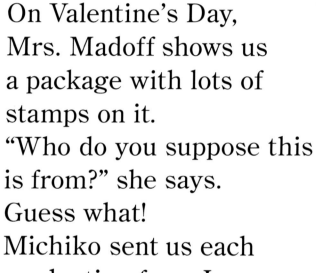

On Valentine's Day,
Mrs. Madoff shows us
a package with lots of
stamps on it.
"Who do you suppose this
is from?" she says.
Guess what!
Michiko sent us each
a valentine from Japan.
They got here just in time.

This is a picture
of me and my
grandmother
and grandfather
in Japan. I've
told them all
about you so they
like you too.
Happy Valentine's Day!
LOVE,
Michixo

Then we each pull a valentine
from the secret box.
"Sam, who's yours from?" Nicholas asks.
"It's from you!" I say.
"And mine is from you!" Nicholas says.

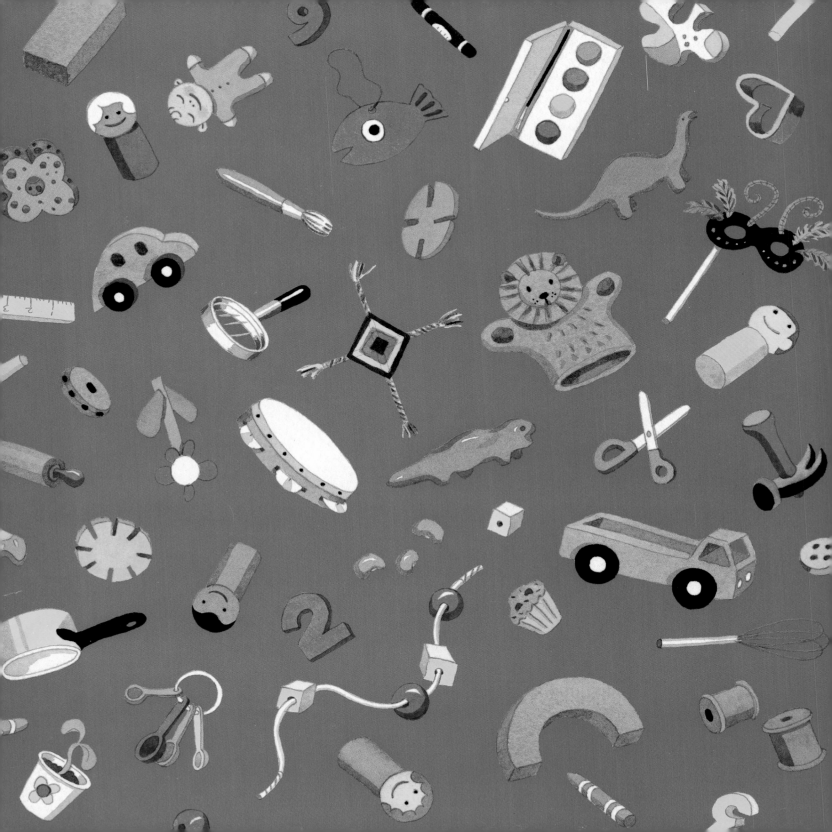